DR AMOL BOSKAVIYA

And Other Stories

AUGUST 16, 2023
SPHERE PUBLICATIONS

By Sarah-Jane Mackenzie

Dr Amol Boskaviya

And Other Stories

'Dr Amol Boskaviya'

At around seven o'clock every evening Dr Amol Boskaviya would try to insist to his wife Sandeen that he should be allowed to wander for approximately an hour around the direction of the Central Lake in Bradford, usually whilst she prepared the main meal.

The time Sandeen had been taking to prepare the main meal had been shortened extensively due to the consideration of Gas Prices lately: though her husband was a rich man she liked, and indeed was expected, to heed the spirit of the collective conscience: and she had even heard rumours that at the main Power Station they had been burning Sylvanian Forests to generate power. She had grown up with occasional trips to York with her Step-mother, who bought her partly to try to make life bearable for her since her own mother had died so cruelly and unexpectedly expensive but truly charming toys from the Fenwick Toy Department: sometimes Beanies, as they were known (charming silkily-furred animals filled with some kind of dried lentils) or plastic toys from the Silvanian Family Range of Animals and Furniture. So Sandeen very much objected to Sylvanian Forests being cut down to enable people to be brainwashed by the Television or to cook a joint of meat.

She had therefore taken to Stir-Frying in a big way. She even coarsely grated potatoes and carrots in order for them to be able to be cooked extra-quickly. She would mix in apples and raisins and a little curry powder, and Dr Amol would always seem full of gratitude for the meals.

Dr Amol was a Child-Psychiatrist. Sometimes he worried that people tended to discriminate against him because he was obviously Asian-looking and still had an Asian-sounding name, though in fact not merely his Father, but his Grandfather too had lived his later life in the UK.

Dr Amol's Grandfather had partly moved away from India because he had objected to the Caste System that had been running very strongly back then (though he had not been born into one of the lower Castes himself), and though Amol agreed with his Ancestor that such discriminative practices were abominable, he preferred to keep marked some affiliation with India, and some degree of separation from many of the fashionable English customs.

In fact Dr Amol talked and berated nightly his current Fellowmen over his extended meals with Sandeen (he would eat very slowly, talk a lot, and often even pause for a while just to look at her in the light of the Candlelight set up in the Dining Room)...about the obvious (in his view) Disassociative Disorder of his fellow Englishmen. The Term had been used lately to describe mainly Females with Split Personalities blameable on some Trauma they had suffered: a de-personalisation and disconnection which made them feel as though they were unreal or that the world about them was unreal...but Dr Amol thought that Men were obviously suffering from the condition too by somehow placing a distance between what they did from day to day and what enabled them to do the things they did.

Somehow they would, for instance, buy cheap ornaments without realising that a special machine must have been adapted to have made them somewhere, and that the materials involved in the making must also have been extracted somehow, by either a machine or a set of people. And then there was the question of Animal Experimentation attached to many of the medicines.

Dr Amol was certainly glad of the Disassociative Disorder in many respects: it would be simply awful if the men around him had thought that they must act like Rambo having seen so many Rambo Films. Some of his own friends had tried to force on him Rambo-Film watching when he had been a Teenager, and that was when he had first decided that if they were going to try and do that to him he would simply avoid the other boys, concentrate almost exclusively on his Studies, and try to find a Relationship with a nice Girl as soon as was possible.

He also liked involving himself with playing the Sitar. The Instrument took a good deal of patience before Mastery was possible, but Dr Amol delighted in the Daily Ritual of Music Practise.

He had so far chosen never to fully consummate his Marriage, and had avoided watching Pornography entirely, ever since a Teacher at his old School had confessed to the Class that he could only ever ejaculate when a woman (whichever woman was not-much of importance) smacked his bottom with a certain frying pan (it had to be the original frying pan, not a stand-in newer model, which also made it not only important that he had to refrain from travel since it was too bulky to fit in a case, but also that no-one but the boys he confessed to would ever know about his sexual preference).

But he loved gently stroking Sandeen's hair and massaging her shoulders and legs, and she would often sit astride him and kiss him passionately, and gently too. He had worriedly observed lately that both of them were going grey, and he feared that the time may have slipped by too quickly: luxurious, but far quicker than he had realised.

Not many other people had ever flirted with Dr Amol, though he was an obviously attractive man, and he was glad to have been faithful in every way he could have been to Sandeen. He hardly ever lost his temper, and he was not a deceitful-type.

However, returning from the Lake that Wednesday Evening he could have sworn, as he entered their smallish Hall Cloakroom, that he could definitely smell the smell of some unaccustomed and unaccounted-for Aftershave on the sleeve of one of Sandeen's Velvet Jackets.

'Epitacio's Auction'

Princeton Brown had no idea how many people would be attending Epitacio's Auction, and he himself hoped that there would be very few other people there. The fewer people there were at an Auction the more likely the prices would be kept down. He was convinced that there might even be some attempts made by some unknown to prevent he himself from attending it. Unusually for the time, there had been an Exhibition of the items in the Church Hall prior to the Auction, and there was a Painting amongst the items that he himself was sure was an item of great worth.

There were some old Military Regalia, and he worried also that the Auction might be prevented because he had seen at the Exhibition there were also some Ivory carvings. He had checked the Local Newspaper afterwards, but there had been nothing said so far.

But after the Exhibition Margaret Slyther, the main Local Librarian, had mentioned some rumour that someone was attending who wished to be the Highest Bidder for all the stock-of-items, every single one of them, who must be a Mad Person, because they wanted badly, it was rumoured, to burn up the lot of it. Every single object. Including the Painting entitled 'The Science Lab'. Princeton had thought that either Margaret had revealed herself as a very eccentric woman, or that it might somehow be in doubt that anyone at all might attend the Auction apart from Epitacio, the Auctioneer, and the few people he might have hired to plant within the Audience. Princeton had suspected for some time, on watching the BBC, that some of the Auctioneers might be planting bit-part Bidders in order to raise prices and interest in items, or even to make a last high-bid if the Auctioneer had decided he might be better off not-selling.

Did Princeton care enough about old objects to try and rumble up the Community to attend to risk their ability for himself to be priced-out on the only item he wanted personally? Because although he suspected that Margaret may be a Liar the Local Community had become in danger of becoming so beaten up with withholding extreme feelings, which he knew really ought to be withheld, but which were boiling over the brim like too much hot jam in too small a pan, he really thought it might be possible that someone might be so enraged that there was evidence there had been a History in Britain, and so consumed by some form of grief, that the alleged Fire-plan might be somewhat indeed a threat.

Princeton knew if he reported the Ivory items the Auction might well be abandoned completely, and if it was known it was he who had reported it, he might be in trouble from Epitacio.

He had marked out 'The Science Lab' Painting as exceptional not only because it was indeed a very finely painted piece, with exceptional detail and representational accuracy in many respects, (but unlikely to be a Digital Fake)....partly because it was rare that Art recognised that Science existed. The Light in the Painting was in places broken into shafts, and there were even chalk-specs in the Atmosphere visible in the area to the side of the Blackboard. He'd also noticed that there were Instruments of Measurement on one of the sage-green counters.

After several glasses of wine Princeton even bordered on the idea of an Anonymous Telephone Call and a Burglary. If he Burgled Epitacio, having made sure that the Auction might be cancelled, Epitacio could presumably claim back some Insurance. If he told Epitacio Margaret Slyther's Story, then Epitacio would know that whomever had made sure that the Auction was cancelled might be doing him a favour and preserving all the items from a risk of savage Fire.

Finally, he decided that all that was not a bad Plan after all, but it would entail a Telephone Call to Epitacio, and his agreement.

And he did not have his number, nor could he find it on the web.

Why would Epitacio have bothered to stage an Exhibition and not even let people know his own Telephone Contact details?

"In the Text Book we're following the Lesson scheduled to be for next Wednesday is all featured around Explanation Myths and Stories, like how the Zebra got his Stripes" Tracey forwarded, sitting back in her chair and abandoning the task somewhat of eating her Vegetarian meal option in order to attempt to interest Colleen, a member of the School Staff who was fairly new to the School, but who was of a reassuringly similar age to herself.

"I'm not going to resist it too much as I think the Folk element to Storytelling is important. But it is important to keep up with new Discoveries and changes to cultural milieu as well. When I was at University I read a lot about Creation Myths, and how they sometimes differed culturally depending on the circumstances to do with the Country in which they originated, though it was surprising how many elements did have similar features across the Literature of the entire World. Sometimes Stories and even Languages are enshrined in the region of their origin and their meaning is untranslatable to people who have not had the same set of experiences. In other cases, there can be really interesting comparisons that may not turn out to be as contrasting as one would have thought."

"For example, the Flood features in not only the Epic of Gilgamesh and the Bible, but in a great deal of the historic Folk Material collected and analysed by many of the Anthropologists in whom I was interested at the time.

"But in some ways I find some of the Stories limited and really very worrying indeed. Would it interrupt the Natural Order too much if they were contested or added to to change them?

"The Roman Myth which originated from a Greek one explaining the Summer and the Winter in terms of the initial Rape of Proserpina and her abduction under ground to live with Pluto affected me with horror and wrath even when I was young and would not have been able to imagine what Rape was, though I knew it must be something really awful....and the fact that every Wintertime afterwards was explained by Pluto's terms that she could leave him every Summer if she returned to the Underworld for Wintertime was a source of worry for me, since some people seemed to even take it for granted that that might not need to be challenged."

"You don't have to try so hard to convince me you might know what you're talking about Tracey. You sound like you're giving me a University Lecture or something....It's ages since we talked, though I admit we haven't talked very often. Less often than I would have liked, in a way. I have been here for two Terms now, and am not even sure some of the other Staff know my name yet. No time anymore for anyone to talk in the Staff Room, and most of the time we're dissuaded from doing so. I've been feeling a bit down recently though, so I might not be very good company." Colleen flicked back her long fringe. Tracey thought it was absurdly long, in fact, particularly for a grey-haired woman. It was as though Colleen was somehow trapped in a time-warp hair-wise of remembering the New Romantic look.

"I remember now feeling really flat and subdued in my childhood," Colleen continued chattering faster than Tracey would think appropriate in a Teacher, and looking down all the time whilst she was talking into the screen of her mobile phone, "and I think it might have been because men were given natural preference back then too. I hate the thought of subduing our Classes more still, when some of the children are hungry and tired again, like I was back then, and vying again with a bullying attitude.

“When I was doing my Teacher Training I remember a story I was told of one young woman who had been very keen to be a Teacher being shocked and upset immensely when one angry Teenager, angry against her for no reason other than to show off to the rest of his friends, and to try and become popular with them I suppose, threw an open bottle of ink all over her clothes. Clothes which she had struggled to afford and which she hoped would have protected her against that kind of awful behaviour.” She hardly paused for breath and Tracey was afraid she might get caught-out not having caught every morsel of the conversation, always fearing she might get trapped by a question later on when her mind had wandered.....

“It was miraculous to some extent how much calmer the Classrooms became when Continuous Assessment elements were used to train and examine the children. But I am worried now they seem to have been scrapped in favour of Examinations again by the current Education Secretary not only that that Classroom calm will disappear further, but that it will be discovered that most of the Teenagers are in fact almost illiterate. They have been getting so used to using Spellcheck Technology on their Computers and so on. And Grammarly. It is likely that it might come to light that none of them can sustain any kind of argument at all when asked to write essays straight out with pen and paper.”

“Are you speaking from experience Colleen? In my Class I have tried to prepare them against the stress of Examinations again by setting them up to write against the clock. I know that that kind of pressure does not suit many of them, but I know too that sometimes practice can help.” Tracey was busy wondering whether Colleen was a snob or a downbeaten woman. She had in her mind been framing things into a series of categories which in some respects she found quite useful sometimes. She thought that Colleen might be more unhappy than she was, she decided.

"I'd invite you out for a drink so we can discuss it further," Colleen offered, "or maybe we could grab a meal at Nando's or something, but I'm under pressure from my In-Laws at home at the moment, besides trying to prepare for my usual Lesson routine.

"They got thrown out of their expensive home because their Business went bust suddenly, and since then have been expecting me to wait on them hand and foot at our house.

"They have the Television on really loud, but seem to also be offended if we don't sit down and watch it with them.

"I can hardly stand it. They don't discuss anything, because it seems as though all the stuffing was knocked out of them with the Business Collapse, and they don't like me much anyway because I never gave them the grand-children they wanted."

"Is the Plan that they will buy a smaller home than their original residence, or are they planning to stay on with you and Derek for some time?" Tracey asked, hoping that she sounded sufficiently tactful.

"To be honest what they are going to do seems like a banned topic with Derek. He doesn't like me trying to establish what is going on and what the future is going to look like for me much at all at the moment. He makes out I am intolerant all the time if I try to direct the conversation into talking about it at all. It's a tricky one about the Zebra though.

"I suppose that with most animals they camouflage, but thinking about it a Zebra's stripes would in some ways give it away even at night. Maybe it's got something to do with a confusion of perspective or something. Funny coincidence actually....Only the other day I saw a female Blackbird treading across some soil that the Council were interfering with for some reason in The Museum

Gardens. I could hardly believe it: the female Blackbird was almost invisible when it was positioned against the soil. I hope there will still be enough worms in it to feed it. Strange how little I know...I suppose it is the Male Blackbird who hunts for worms and things though....Is it? Thinking about the camouflage I did wonder whether the Female Blackbird does look out and hunt a little for some of her Community also, though I suppose she can't be the one looking for the worms whilst she is keeping the new-born chicks warm in the nest...can she?" Colleen suddenly looked not only perplexed but tearful. She smoothed both brows with her fingers, but the forming tears were nevertheless not prevented.

"Did you really want children of your own Colleen?" Tracey asked as gently and tentatively as she could manage.

"It's great guiding my Pupils. Maybe if I'd had children of my own I wouldn't have become a Teacher."

"I would disagree with you somewhat about the Zebras." Tracey offered, in a continuation of the other thread with diversionary intent. "If a Lion or Tiger is crouched down seeing through the grass the yellow-coloured grass might make stripes and it might be somewhat difficult therefore to make out a Zebra."

"But the whole thing is loaded in favour of the Predator. The Lion is, and would be, gold-coloured like the grass. Why allow it so much camouflage against the interests of the innocents?"

"If you are trying to make out that the World is generally balanced in favour of evil I have to object." Tracey replied, pulling a determined frown with emphasis, and grabbing up her bag from beside her chair with an air of determined chagrin, before marching out of the Dining Room.

****

It was some days later when Tracey was leading a Group of Teenagers down the main corridor to Assembly, making sure they had their Instruments with them as that day they were due to Play in front of the School a Folk Song that Gordon, the Music Teacher, had composed a new tune to (ruining it in Tracey's view), - when Colleen, passing the other way perhaps in order to call in at the Cloakroom before the event, suddenly called out as she passed more loudly than Tracey would have liked, and certainly louder than she had ever heard Colleen before

"And How would you Rescue Proserpina?"

Tracey was somewhat annoyed and yet flattered to an extent that her question had hit a nerve...but inconvenienced by the circumstances of the situation also. She was clearly busy. She really would not have wanted to raise the question of Proserpina with the Teenagers around her at all. And it was not even clear whether Colleen was expecting a reply, or expecting there to be no suitable reply....or whether she was in fact herself in the midst of a Nervous Breakdown....a condition which was feared greatly amongst the Staff, as they all feared that if they had one they wouldn't ever get a further Job Offer, and probably wouldn't even be allowed time off to recuperate.

In the end she decided to try to quickly reply as assertively as she could, gesturing with her hands held back at a wide angle for the small crowd around her to pause whilst she dealt with the question.

"I think I would try to foil Pluto into thinking a look-alike Robot was a preferable option for him, and sneak Proserpina away from Hades whilst he was distracted with it."

The answer seemed to satisfy Colleen's immediate need, and she smiled wanly before flicking her fringe and pacing off again towards the Washroom. Had she been drinking? Tracey wondered.....

*****

"The Floral Dance" just didn't seem right to a different tune....Why spoil something that was refreshingly good in the first place? Though the Teenagers did a marvellous job of it for the most part, and Tracey could tell that Gordon was proud of them. Jessie sang the whole Song wonderfully to the new tune, with lyrics about Cornwall that Tracey had not really been aware of when the Song to the Original Tune had come out into the Charts in the Eighties. The light of the Sun was on her hair as she sang, making it look vibrant.

Gordon had been talking to her recently about the way that he feared that a lot of young people had been encouraged to give up on any hope of being taught how to actually read Music. He had expressed his absolute determination that his own Pupils would not be treated so unfairly. Fortunately, the Head-Master had backed him with his Idealism, and somehow funding had been arranged and negotiated to get the Music Department fitted up with proper Instruments that the children could loan if they were learning Music with Gordon.

Tracey liked Gordon, but she really found herself with quite strong objections to the fact that "The Floral Dance" was not sung to the original tune. She was perhaps developing Superstitions in her older age, and she sometimes thought that some of the better older Music and Poetry was composed like some kind of Charm, to try and keep the Natural Order of things running in a way that was beneficent. With regard to a great deal of the older Poetry and Folk Songs she did object to their obvious Sexism: she had to think that things could indeed be changed for the better, and had in some areas definitely experienced changes for the better. But some of the older Music was definitely infused with a Kind kind of Witchcraft, she thought.

Her Uncle had once bought her a Record of Mary O'Hara singing "The Floral Dance" amongst some other haunting melodies, with undoubted power. She still had an old Record Player, and played the record very seldom because she thought that recognition was needed of the fact that though it had been so popular, featured on Adverts on TV and so on, which might in a way make it seem neutralised of Magic, that it was indeed Magic and should be played only when the Ritual of Magic was needed, to listen to with solemn attention.

Tracey had begun to think that Magic was certainly, though frightening to her, an area that might need addressing: partly because so many of the younger generation had been brought up either reading, or watching, Tales to do with Harry Potter.

It was obvious to her that to some extent that might have culturally affected the children...and she was particularly worried about rather nasty sadistic people thinking that they might form some kind of legitimised Gang, like the Slytherine House in Harry Potter.

Those kinds of worries made her partly of the camp of those who had objected to Harry Potter when it was first written, and who had tried to argue that there might be some kind of worryingly anti-Christian elements to the Stories.

She knew that a lot of the Teenagers she had already taught had over time been lured into buying Spellbooks to do with finding a boyfriend and somehow chanting at the Moon along with using BodyShop products to try and make things run a little smoother for them. Most of the Mothers had assumed that all the Spellbooks were obviously of limited or even no Magical power in reality, but that they were mostly a commercial enterprise...but Tracey knew that in some ways the Commercial traps were getting worse for young girls and women, and that some of them were experimenting quite a lot to try and recreate a sense of Natural Romance into their World.

'The Green Glass Vase'

(A Story in a similar style to Hans Christian-Anderson's 'The Iron Street Lamp', and set with reference to Victorian Times)

"You are not such a lovely-looking green glass vase" the copper kettle whistled. "I can see where you've been repaired".

"I was well worth repairing."

"I am a lovely kettle. I have to keep telling myself that. I need to keep believing in myself, that's all. Have you been here long?"

"Months."

"I don't understand why neither of us has been bought yet. We are both set at ridiculously cheap prices."

"You have only been here a day! We must wait and be patient. That is all we can do. Wait, and hope. They do not realize just how valuable I am and I fear I will be thrown away tomorrow"

"I fear we will be thrown away tomorrow too. I am lonely. My owner just died. They cleared his house and I have been separated from all my old companions and brought here whereas they have been taken to auction I think. It smells fusty in this shop and I do not think everything is very clean. I feel nervous. The wind isn't helping my nerves. I keep imagining everything blown away – a great wind carrying everything across the plain and devastating the area, the whole lot. I half want it to, I am so cross and frightened for myself."

"Then whilst it is dark and there are no customers I will tell you my story. Let's keep each other company whilst the wind whistles outside on this stormy night and tomorrow maybe we will both get bought by some nice people. At least the money will be towards a good cause.

"But they have overlooked me for months. I think the big lady that manages this charity shop is going to move some of us on and possibly throw us out into the skip soon. I've seen her do it to other ornaments that do not get bought."

"I did not realize our time here might be the end."

"It is a pity. They do not realize I am a magic vase and a very valuable item indeed."

"You're not magic. I am great. I am shiny. You are just a plain old green vase."

"Well listen to my story at least. Tomorrow I may be gone for good, as you say. Tomorrow I may be thrown in the skip with the rest of the rubbish and the old damp clothes that the Manager thinks no one would buy."

"OK – I'll listen, but you can't pull the wool over my eyes. I am a very sassy copper kettle. I will be able to tell if you're lying, you know. But tell us your story and we will discuss it afterwards if there is still time in store, if you will forgive the pun."

"Listen then and save your judgement until afterwards. It will soon enough be dawn.

A long time ago in the North of England there lived a young woman called Gladdys whose mother died of tuberculosis, and whose father died as well shortly afterwards. She herself and her two brothers were grief-stricken, but they managed to keep their tears to a moderate level at the father's funeral (though Gladdys had had to be taken out of her mother's because she had had difficulty controlling her tears) and fortunately their father had been quite rich – so they all looked forward to a share of his money and his possessions through his will.

Gladdys hoped that she would be well provided for – but when the day came she was shocked to find that though her father had left his house to one of her brothers and his money to the other – all he had instructed the solicitor to arrange for she herself – all he had bequeathed – was a green glass vase – ME - along with a letter that was not to be opened until her 21st birthday.

She remembered she had admired me as a young girl and that her mother had told her her grandmother had given me to the couple on the occasion of their wedding day. When she was just a young girl Gladdys had used to gather flowers for her mother from the large garden and her mother had used to put them in me – a lovely, if I say so myself, absolutely glorious, green glass vase. But Gladdys's feelings towards me had always been ambiguous because at first the flowers had always looked lovely, then they would wane and finally the flowers in me would have to be thrown away and changed. She'd never known as a young girl whether she wouldn't have preferred to leave them in the garden. I once remember her with her face all cross and scrunched up in tears because of all that. The large white daisies she had been trying to draw had changed position overnight and wilted significantly – it frustrated her so much she was so upset .... that I was afraid she would smash me then and there.

Anyway, everybody did assume that the letter would contain some instruction to provide her with an adequate living, including the men who courted her and David who finally married her just three months before the letter was due to be opened.

He wanted to go with her to the solicitors on her 21st birthday but when the day came they had a terrible argument and Gladdys stormed off by herself, telling him she did not want his company and fully assuming that she was about to come into some money in her own right. The solicitor, Mr Gerrard, handed over the letter) with a slight smile and a great deal of formality. Gladdys found she was nervous about opening it, but eventually, her mouth dry and heart beating rapidly, with quivering hands she broke the seal and opened the vellum envelope. It had the address of a station deposit box in it – and it said she was to ask for the key for it from the solicitor. That puzzled and alarmed her a little because surely her father would not have left a lot of money in a station deposit box. She had had not even known that people were allowed to store things there for so long a time. But to complicated things further the station was further North in Edinburgh.

She wondered whether she should try to make it up with David. She began to be nervous that she might not have a great amount of money bequeathed to her after all, and was worried how he too might react to that fact. He had definitely thought he had won the competition of suitors with that prize in mind, she knew, because she had played on it and flirted with them all with that aura of a cash or property promise flaunted mischievously before them all. What was he going to say now?

She was too nervous about it to go home to his house – that had become hers too perhaps on that flimsy understanding. It was possible he did not love her at all. He had just perhaps loved beating out all the other people she had had around her competing for her hand in marriage. And she had realized already that she did not love him. He was mean, and cross-tempered, and far too demanding.

So she sought out her Aunt who lived in Scarborough and confided in her. Aunt Helen calmed Gladdys's tears and assured her she should not fear for her future too much. She knew of a couple that were looking for a live-in Governess for their young girl Rosemary. She suggested that Gladdys could pretend she was not married at all, could fake a new name if there was no money and she did not love her husband – as she suspected was the case. They would sort it out, she said.

Aunt Helen said she would travel along with Gladdys to the station with the safe deposit box the very next day. She said there was no use fretting about it and dreading it – it was something that they had to do and that they would do together and that the sooner they found out what the situation actually was, the better the situation would be, even if it was only for the knowing of it.

So the very next day they travelled together by train to Edinburgh Station and found box no 12. The key certainly fitted, at least.

But inside there was only a book. A newish-looking one at that. Leather-bound. With a picture of a daisy embossed on the cover.

Gladdys was so appalled and distraught that she did not even open the book for some days. There were after all plenty of other things now that had to be taken care of. She had to find a way of making a living because she knew that David would be so furious and disappointed that he would make their married life even more miserable for her than it had already been -even if he consented to take her back – and for that she would now have to plead, she knew, and she did not want to. She wanted to retain her pride. She changed her name from Gladdys O'Brien to Violet Evans and applied for the position to teach Rosemary. Fortunately the girl's mother took an immediate liking to her and did not ask her too many questions.

When Gladdys did open the book, a few months later, she found that it seemed to be just a book of herbal remedies that she was not sure would work or not. But in the very central pages of the book she found something rather different.

It was a spell that claimed that once it was bestowed upon a vase, the cut flowers in the vase would never wilt or die but would last forever. Great news for me, you understand

But she was even more sceptical about that than she was about the remedies – and it was only after she had cured herself from the flu - using one of them in desperation, that she suddenly realized the spell might work too, and might be fun at least to try.

The instructions said she had to prepare candles in a circle and place me in the middle and chant some words and throw some rose petals over me. She did everything that the book said she had to because she was curious and needed cheering up and thought it would divert her a little bit to delve into the exploration of whether this bequeathed spell actually worked or not. (Rosemary was proving to be a bit of a difficult and awkward child, dreadfully spoilt and difficult to teach).

Once the ceremony was in place, hearing her chant at first it felt silly but then I felt strange and giddy, as though I was going to shatter. Then, suddenly, I was almost overcome by a surge of vigour so great that it was almost overwhelming. There was a sudden pulse of bright light, then just as suddenly and even more inexplicably dark all around and silence as we waited in shock. I could feel myself all fizzing with power and strength.

I could not wait to see myself if I was transformed to a magical object and could keep flowers alive in me for always and indeed I did not have to wait to see for very long.

Gladdys placed some graceful white lillies in me.

Well, I have to say and I am very pleased to say, that the lillies lasted, and lasted, and kept beautiful through all of that winter, through the hail, through the snow, even through the frost and withstood the draughts.... and the smell of the fresh lillies permeated throughout the house.

Gladdys had the idea of making 10 more vases magical in the same way as me – through the spell in the book.

She sold the rest of them and kept me – but with the money she sold them for she was able to secure her own future and become an artist as she had always wanted.

Sometimes she would change the flowers in me just for a change. Tulips, Chrysanthemums, Hydrangeas, Daffodils - And she would paint and paint, and my powers would be loyal and magical and the flowers did not wilt or change but held steady as she applied layer after layer of oil paint to her masterworks.

She was always frightened lest I get broken and was very careful with me - but then one day a scruffy little boy who had come to collect some brushes for his mother knocked me off the windowsill by accident and I fell onto the floor and a small triangle piece chipped off me round my rim.

Gladdys was most upset. She shouted at the boy in anger and he flew out of the house frightened.

She pasted the fragment of glass back onto me, making me whole once more - but my powers were lost. She watched some tulips die and with great sadness and resignation put me back in a glass cupboard near the window.

She had sold the other magical vases she had made and the book with the spell in it had been burned in a fire some years ago – so she thought the eternal flowers were gone for ever from the world never to return except in her memories, her paintings and her dreams.

But bit by bit and year by year I began to recover. I could gradually feel my energy rising again. I thought it may be just a matter of time before my powers were completely restored.

Sadly though I watched my mistress die. She had made some money and a reputation for herself through her paintings but gradually began to lose heart over the years, being lonely, I think.

She got up later and later each day and went to bed earlier and earlier each night. I wished I could give her pleasure again. She had neglected to even try out my powers believing they were lost forever and I stood neglected still in the glass cupboard near the window. I wished I could reinvigorate her too – it was terrible seeing her slumped dead form in front of me at her chair – she was all in a white nightgown, as white as the lillies she had first put in me ...but this time I was powerless.

Rosemary, her niece, took a liking to me even though I was damaged.

An American soldier courted her, and one evening brought her a beautiful bunch of yellow roses. That was the night they kissed. She put them inside me and I kept them for her – trying hard to remember what it was like to have been magical and hoping I was magical again. I could smell their sweet scent and wanted it to last.

My powers were fully restored because those yellow roses stayed fresh for fifty years until she died, though the young man who gave her them was killed in the war just a couple of months after they were selected. Rosemary became poor when her father lost all the family money through gambling , but she was too sentimental towards me and those roses ever to part with me.

But when she did pass away I myself passed then into the hands of a Mr Talporch who soon learned of my powers and determined that what he should do with me was to store flower seeds inside me, not flowers at all – in the hope that the seeds too would keep an everlasting power.

He was seeing how the natural world around him was changing fast and faring for the worse and that land was being taken over by businesses, the green fields with tar, the cities ever-expanding.

If he thought a flower was rare, either a wild flower or a garden flower, he would put some seeds for that flower inside me – just a few – but enough, he thought, for it to end up a valuable collection.

But he knew that the longer he held onto his asset and the worse things became for the wildlife the more of a valuable asset the seed selection would become.

There was a real danger though that he might leave it too late for any of the seeds to be able to thrive once they were planted.

As fortune would have it he was killed one day in a car accident before he either sowed the seeds or realized the sum of money he had been hoping to gain from them.

A young vicar called Alan found me full of the seeds and immediately sowed them in the local Churchyard (about the only green space let).

But he did not realize my powers and put me in a box with other bits and pieces and sent me here, to the Charity shop, where I am now priced at £1.50p, where everybody is unaccountably ignoring me."

"That is a very strange story, but it has kept me entertained I admit" said the copper kettle. "I am not sure I believe a word of it but Maybe when the shop opens you will get bought".

"Maybe I will."

"I will tell you my own story tomorrow and you will be even more amazed."

"It's a deal". They both got a bit of sleep and looked forward to the key rattling in the lock.

But the next day the plump Manager was squeezing by the circular clothes stand near the ornaments section when she knocked the green glass vase off the shelf entirely. There was nothing anybody could do. There was a crash and the green glass vase shattered into thousands of pieces. The Manager, Dawn, shrugged her shoulders with an air of impatience and emotional withdrawal and gave a brisk call for someone with a sweeping brush.

And that night, when all the people had gone home again and the lights had been switched off in the shop the copper kettle screamed with force and shivered with loneliness. The clothes whispered a muffled retort and the moon rays shone in through the window. Occasionally the shop's contents heard a bus passing with a loud trundle, and the wailing of a siren indicating more trouble, but some help across the dark expanse outside and within the emptiness of each troubled heart.

Dawn came and the key rattled in the door at 8 am as usual. The shop doors opened an 9 am.

At 12 noon they had a visitor. A very well-to-do lady with a bright orange headscarf who said that she was about to donate a grand picture to the shop worth thousands of thousands. She would have it sold at auction and the profit would go to the charity. With some enthusiasm she showed the Manager a photo of the painting.

In the photo the Manager was rather unnerved to see standing once more the very same green glass vase she had seen around the shop for months, with some beautiful graceful white lillies inside it and a silver moon in the blue-grey sky.

'The Art Match-Bureau'

Serena was thinking about the idea of setting up a Match-making Bureau which matched people in accordance with which style of Art they preferred. She didn't really know whether she would ever get to actually be able to own or rent a Building for her Enterprise, or whether it would ever take off or not, seeing as though she had no Capital of Cash to invest, and the Country was currently in a state of recession, with Banks not eager to lend money at all, particularly not to women. But she remembered how enchanted she had been as a young girl, leafing through Magazines which showed Brides in their beautiful Wedding Dresses, and which even talked about complete Marketing Fairs in Birmingham in which such items were displayed, and from which young women could choose, with the reality being that their Marriages would indeed be worthwhile, and a pleasure and happiness for both parties, and children too later on. So since she was not in work at the moment, and since she had already a Doctorate in Sociology, she thought she might as well spend her time dreaming and Planning nevertheless.

'The Impressionists' had been talked about a lot during her twenties, and were for some the only Artists they had ever had a real awareness of. And Damien Hirst also. Tracey Emin had been talked about, but it would be probably unwise to Match a Couple on the basis of liking a bed which proved forms of mass-exploitation and intentions to derange. Personally, she could not stand Picasso, and would have been suspicious of any man who might prefer a woman to have cone-like pointy breasts and half a face, though she knew that in part Madonna (the Pop Star) had played into that styling. Even with the Impressionists it really would depend on which of the Impressionist Artists you liked most: Degas might indicate a future child-Abuser.

In fact, the more she thought about it, the more she realised it ought to have been the woman providing the picture. But even as recently as The Impressionists there had been few acclaimed Female Artists, and the few of them there were might have been more interested in apeing Male ones, perhaps in comment, perhaps in order to try and attain similar notice, rather in outlining their own Vision of what they might hope another too would aspire towards, or value.

Serena was not a Lesbian, but she had not successfully found anyone in the world who seemed to share her own hopes, or who might be willing to spend some time with her and share conversations and exchange opinions. She had slept with a number of men, but having conversations obviously had not been part of their own Plans. She knew that many of the older Generation said that as far as their own marriages went they passed each other like Ships in the Night: maybe also indicating that they were too tired by their separate working lives to interact at all, except from an automatic pilot habitual awareness and annoyance.

The first thing she obviously had to do was find a Female Artist who she herself liked and would want to promote and have recognised with reverence somewhat......

Printed in Great Britain
by Amazon

33442008R00020